THE PANJANDRUM
OF TOBOKU

Or, Gilbert & Sullivan's Masterpiece
for Modern Sensitivities

Any racial and ethnic overtones can remain only in awareness of the original show, which is beyond any human pen to correct.

THE PANJANDRUM OF TOBOKU

PHYLLIS ANN KARR

WILDSIDE PRESS

Published by Wildside Press LLC.
wildsidepress.com | bcmystery.com

AUTHOR'S NOTE

While hoping that any group wishing to mount this version will purchase enough copies for everyone who needs one, I should like to offer it otherwise royalty-free to school, university, and other amateur groups, especially those that specialize in G&S for the love of the Savoy series. (A DVD or CD would be nice, but not requisite, in return.)

If, during my lifetime, a professional or semi-pro group should wish to mount it with a view to turning any substantial profit (beyond operating expenses and survival of the company in question), the shade of W. S. Gilbert would not let me rest without asking something for my work. Please contact me through my publisher.

NOTE

During my lifetime, I have seen well-to-do People of Color glee-fully collecting vintage bric-a-brac that in the days of their parents and grandparents would have fueled race riots. I can bravely predict that in another generation or two, when I am no longer around to see it, The Mikado *will be rediscovered and gleefully performed as its authors envisioned it, with everyone—including Japanese—wondering what all the fuss was about. Meanwhile, those of us who love G&S scrabble for ways to save perhaps the biggest box-office draw in our repertory (rivaled only by* Pinafore*).*

We recognize that it might be futile. Likely the Japanese tie-in was among the elements that made The Mikado *such a block-buster in its own day. And perhaps awareness of what the show traditionally was remains too raw a wound for* any *bandage whatever to suffice for a generation or two. Yet we scrabble on.*

This, then, is one more effort to render Gilbert & Sullivan's masterpiece racially and ethnically inoffensive. Unable to see how simply changing the national or ethnic group can solve the problem, I have tried turning the story openly into the province of Gilbert's fantasy Topsyturvydom that it always was beneath its pseudo-Japanese mask, as were Pinafore *and the others beneath their British (or, exceptionally, Venetian, Utopian, and Pfenig Halbpfennigan) veneers.*

SETTING

The fantasy realm of Toboku. *There should be absolutely no far Eastern (Japanese or Chinese) elements in either costumes or scenery. (If your umwelt would tolerate the suggestion, why not do the ever-lovin' Real Thing?)*

DRAMATIS PERSONAE

The Grand Panjandrum of Toboku
Chico, the Lord High Executioner
Lord Prufrock
Lord Factotum
Handy Lou
Trillium *(accent on second syllable when rhythm requires)*
Pattycake
Prissy
Nattyshaw

PROLOGUE (OPT.)

Delivered by any character in front of the curtain

So she went into the garden to cut a cabbage leaf, to make an apple pie;

And at the same time a great she-bear coming up the street, pops its head into the shop.

"What! no soap?" So he died,

And she very imprudently married the barber;

And there were present the Loblilies, and the Joblillies, and the Garyulies,

And the grand Panjandrum himself, with the little round button at top;

And they all fell to playing the game of catch as catch can,

Till the gunpowder ran out at the heels of their boots.

> (attributed to Samuel Foote, 1720-1777;
> "Picninnies" rev. to "Loblilies")

ACT I

MALE CHORUS. *(tune: "The Soldiers of the Queen" from Patience.)[1]*

The men of Toboku
Before you now assemble.
To our Panjandrum true[2]
We always bow and tremble.
But when his gaze is elsewhere,
We love to cut our capers,
Of fun to have our full share,
And read our daily papers. *(They open newspapers.)*

(Enter HANDY LOU.)

RECITATIVE—HANDY LOU

Gentlemen, I pray you tell me
Where a gentle maiden dwelleth
Named Trillium, the ward of Chico?
In pity speak—oh, speak, I pray you!

FACTOTUM. Why, who are you who ask this question?
HANDY LOU. Come, gather round me, and I'll tell you.

SONG—HANDY LOU and MEN'S CHORUS

A Wandering minstrel I—
    A thing of shreds and patches,
    Of ballads, songs, and snatches,
And dreamy lullaby.

---

1   "If You Want to Know Who We Are" and "Miya Sama" are the *ONLY* two musical numbers to have been replaced.

2   Or, if you want to go that way with make-up and/or costuming, "blue."

My catalogue is long,
    Through every passion ranging,
    And to your humors changing
I tune my supple song!

    Are you in sentimental mood?
        I'll sigh with you,
            Oh, sorrow!
    On maiden's coldness do you brood?
        I'll do so, too—
            Oh, sorrow, sorrow!
    I'll charm your willing ears
    With songs of lovers' fears,
    While sympathetic tears
        My cheeks bedew—
            Oh, sorrow, sorrow!

But if patriotic sentiment is wanted,
    I've patriotic ballads cut and dried;
For where'er our country's banner may be planted,
    All other local banners are defied!
Our warriors, in serried ranks assembled,
    Never quail—or they conceal it if they do—
And I shouldn't be surprised if nations trembled
    Before the mighty troops of Toboku!

CHORUS. We shouldn't be surprised, etc.

HAND. And if you call for a song of the sea,
    We'll heave the capstan round,
With a yeo heave ho, for the wind is free,
Her anchor's a-trip and her helm's a-lee,
    Hurrah for the homeward bound!

CHOR.   Yeo-ho—heave-ho—
    Hurrah for the homeward bound!

HAND. To lay aloft in a howling breeze
    May tickle a landsman's taste,

But the happiest hour a sailor sees
       Is when he's down
       At an inland town,
With his Nancy on his knees, yeo-ho!
    And his arm around her waist!

CHOR.   Then man the capstan—off we go,
        As the fiddler swings us round,
    With a yeo heave ho,
    And a rumbelow,
        Hurrah for the homeward bound!

HAND. A wandering minstrel I, etc.

FACT. And what may be your business with Trillium?

HAND. I'll tell you. A year ago I was a member of your town band. It was my duty to take the cap round for contributions. While discharging this delicate office, I saw Trillium. We loved each other at once, but she was betrothed to her guardian Chico, a cheap tailor, and I saw that my suit was hopeless. Overwhelmed with despair, I quitted your town. Judge of my delight when I heard, a month ago, that Chico had been condemned to death for flirting! I hurried back at once, in the hope of finding Trillium at liberty to listen to my protestations.

FACT. It is true that Chico was condemned to death for flirting, but he was reprieved at the last moment, and raised to the exalted rank of Lord High Executioner under the following remarkable circumstances:

SONG—FACTOTUM and CHORUS

FACT. Our great Panjandrum, virtuous man,
When he to rule our land began,
    Resolved to try
    A plan whereby
  Young men might best be steadied.
So he decreed, in words succinct,
That all who flirted, leered, or winked

(Unless connubially linked),
  Should forthwith be beheaded.
And I expect you'll all agree
That he was right to so decree.
      And I am right,
      And you are right,
And all is right as right can be!

CHOR.   And you are right,
      And we are right, etc.

FACT.   This stern decree, you'll understand,
Caused great dismay throughout the land!
      For young and old
      And shy and bold
  Were equally affected.
The youth who winked a roving eye,
Or breathed a non-connubial sigh,
Was thereupon condemned to die—
      He usually objected.

      And you'll allow, as I expect,
      That he was right to so object.
            And I am right,
            And you are right,
      And everything is quite correct!

CHOR.   And you are right,
      And we are right, etc.

FACT.   And so we straight let out on bail
A convict from the county jail.
      Who head was next
      On some pretext
  Condem-ned to be mown off,
And made *him* Headsman, for we said,
"Who's next to be decapited
Cannot cut off another's head
      Until he's cut his own off."

And we are right, I think you'll say,
To argue in this kind of way;
    And I am right,
    And you are right,
And all is right—too-looral-lay!

CHOR.   And you are right,
          And we are right, etc.

(Exeunt CHORUS. Enter LORD PRUFROCK.)

HAND. Chico, the cheap tailor, Lord High Executioner? Why, that's the highest rank a citizen can attain!

PRU. It is. Our logical Panjandrum, seeing no moral difference between the dignified judge who condemns a criminal to die, and the industrious mechanic who carries out the sentence, has rolled the two offices into one, and every judge is now his own executioner.

HAND. But how good of you (for I see that you are a nobleman of the highest rank) to condescend to tell all this to me, a mere strolling minstrel!

PRU. Don't mention it. I am, in point of fact, a particularly haughty and exclusive person, of pre-Adamite ancestral descent. You will understand this when I tell you that I can trace my ancestry back to a protoplasmal primordial atomic globule. Consequently, my family pride is something inconceivable. I can't help it. I was born sneering. But I struggle hard to overcome this defect. I mortify my pride continually. When all the great officers of State resigned in a body because they were too proud to serve under an ex-tailor, did I not unhesitatingly accept all their posts at once?

FACT. And the salaries attached to them. You did.

PRU. It is consequently my degrading duty to serve this upstart as First Lord of the Treasury, Lord Chief Justice, Commander-in-Chief, Lord High Admiral, Master of the Buckhounds, Groom of the Back Stairs, Archbishop of Toboku, and Lord Mayor, both acting and elect, all rolled into one. And at a salary! A Prufrock paid for his services! I a salaried minion! But

I do it! It revolts me, but I do it!

HAND. And it does you credit.

PRU. But I don't stop at that. I go and dine with middle-class people on reasonable terms. I dance at cheap suburban parties for a moderate fee. I accept refreshment at any hands, however lowly. I also retail State secrets at a very low figure. For instance, any further information about Trillium would come under the head of a State secret. *(HANDY LOU takes the hint and gives him money.) (Aside.)* Another insult, and, I think, a light one!

SONG—PRUFROCK with HANDY LOU and FACTOTUM

PRU. Young man, despair,
    Likewise go to.
Trillium the fair
    You must not woo.
    It will not do:
    I'm sorry for you,
You very imperfect ablutioner!
This very day
    From school Trillium
Will wend her way,
    And homeward come,
    With beat of drum
    And a rum-tum-tum,
To wed the Lord High Executioner!
    And the brass will crash,
        And the trumpets bray,
    And they'll cut a dash
        On their wedding day.
She'll toddle away, as all aver,
With the Lord High Executioner!

HAND. and **FACT.**   And the brass will crash, etc.

ALL.   She'll toddle away, etc.

PRU.   It's a hopeless case,

As you may see,
And in your place,
Away I'd flee;
But don't blame me—
I'm sorry to be
Of your pleasure a diminutioner.
They'll vow their pact
Extremely soon,
In point of fact
This afternoon.
Her honeymoon
With that buffoon
At seven commences, so *you* shun her!

HAND. and **FACT.**   And the brass will crash, etc.

ALL.   She'll toddle away, etc.

(Exit FACTOTUM.)

RECITATIVE—HANDY LOU and PRUFROCK

HAND. And have I journeyed for a month, or nearly,
To learn that Trillium, whom I love so dearly,
This day to Chico is to be united?
PRU. The fact appears to be as you've recited.
But here he comes, equipped as suits his station;
He'll give you any further information.

(Enter MEN'S CHORUS.)

CHOR. Behold the Lord High Executioner!
A personage of noble rank and title—
A dignified and potent officer,
Whose functions are particularly vital!
Defer, defer,
To the Lord High Executioner!

(Enter CHICO.)

SOLO—CHICO with CHORUS

Taken from the county jail
    By a set of curious chances;
Liberated then on bail,
    On my own recognizances;
Wafted by a favoring gale
    As one sometimes is in trances,
To a height that few can scale,
    Save by long and weary dances;
Surely never had a male
    Under suchlike circumstances
So adventurous a tale,
    Which may rank with most romances.

CHOR. Taken from the county jail, etc.
    Defer, defer,
To the Lord High Executioner, etc.

CHICO. Gentlemen, I'm much touched by this reception. I can only trust that by strict attention to duty I shall ensure a continuance of those favors which it will ever be my study to deserve. If I should ever be called upon to act professionally, I am happy to think that there will be no difficulty in finding plenty of people whose loss will be a distinct gain to society at large.

SOLO—CHICO with CHORUS

CHIC. As some day it may happen that a victim must be found,
    I've got a little list—I've got a little list
Of society offenders who might well be underground,
    And who never would be missed—who never would be
missed!
    There's the pestilential nuisances who write for autographs—
    All people who have flabby hands and irritating laughs—
    All children who are up in dates, and floor you with 'em flat—
    All persons who in shaking hands, shake hands with you like
that—
    And all third persons who on spoiling *tete-a-tetes* insist—
    They'd none of 'em be missed—they'd none of 'em be
missed!

CHOR. He's got 'em on the list—he's got 'em on the list;
And they'll none of 'em be missed—they'll none of 'em be missed.

CHIC. There's all the athletes who insist they won't take second place,
    And the croaky vocalist—I've got him on the list!
And the people who eat peppermint and puff it in your face,
    They never would be missed—they never would be missed!
Then the idiot who praises, with enthusiastic tone,
All centuries but this, and every country but his own;
And the lady from the provinces, who dresses like a guy,
And who "doesn't think she dances, but would rather like to try"!
And that singular anomaly, the lady novelist[3]—
    I don't think she's be missed—I'm *sure* she'd not be missed!

CHOR. He's got her on the list—he's got her on the list;
And I don't think she'll be missed—I'm *sure* she'll not be missed!

CHIC. And that *Nisi Prius* nuisance, who just now is rather rife,
    The Judicial humorist—I've got *him* on the list![4]
All funny fellows, comic men, and clowns of private life—
    They'd none of 'em be missed—they'd none of 'em be missed.
And apologetic statesmen of a compromising kind,
Such as—What d'ye call him—Thing'em-bob, and likewise—Never-mind,
And 'St—'st—'st—and What's-his-name, and also You-know-who—
    The task of filling up the blanks I'd rather leave to *you*.

---

3   As a lady novelist myself, I always feel cheated when this verse is changed—especially when changed to "the girl who's never kissed, which is several degrees more cruel. We *choose* to publish novels, and must take our chances; but who—especially when young—would ever choose to repel the complementary sex?

4   Surely *Trial by Jury* and *Iolanthe* qualify Gilbert himself as a judicial humorist.

But it really doesn't matter whom you put upon the list,
    For they'd none of 'em be missed—they'd none of 'em be missed!

    CHOR. You may put 'em on the list—you may put 'em on the list;
    And they'll none of 'em be missed—they'll none of 'em be missed!

(Exeunt CHORUS.)

(Enter PRUFROCK.)

CHIC. Prufrock, it seems that the festivities in connection with my approaching marriage must last a week. I should like to do it handsomely, and I want to consult you as to the amount I ought to spend upon them.

PRU. Certainly. In which of my capacities? As First Lord of the Treasury, Lord Chamberlain, Attorney-General, Chancellor of the Exchequer, Privy Purse, or Private Secretary?

CHIC. Suppose we say as Private Secretary.

PRU. Speaking as your Private Secretary, I should say that, as the city will have to pay for it, don't stint yourself, do it well.

CHIC. Exactly—as the city will have to pay for it. That is your advice.

PRU. As Private Secretary. Of course you will understand that, as Chancellor of the Exchequer, I am bound to see that due economy is observed.

CHIC. Oh! But you said just now, "Don't stint yourself, do it well."

PRU. As Private Secretary.

CHIC. And now you say that due economy must be observed.

PRU. As Chancellor of the Exchequer.

CHIC. I see. Come over here, where the Chancellor can't hear us. *(They cross the stage.)* Now, as my Solicitor, how do you advise me to deal with this difficulty?

PRU. Oh, as your Solicitor, I should have no hesitation in saying, "Chance it—"

CHIC. Thank you. *(Shaking his hand.)* I will.

PRU. If it were not that, as Lord Chief Justice, I am bound to see that the law isn't violated.

CHIC. I see. Come over here where the Chief Justice can't hear us. *(They cross the stage.)* Now, then, as First Lord of the Treasury?

PRU. Of course, as First Lord of the Treasury, I could propose a special vote that would cover all expenses, if it were not that, as Leader of the Opposition, it would be my duty to resist it, tooth and nail. Or, as Paymaster-General, I could so cook the accounts that, as Lord High Auditor, I should never discover the fraud. But then, as Archbishop of Toboku, it would be my duty to denounce my dishonesty and give myself into my own custody as First Commissioner of Police.

CHIC. That's extremely awkward.

PRU. I don't say that all these distinguished people couldn't be squared; but it is right to tell you that they wouldn't be sufficiently degraded in their own estimation unless they were insulted with a very considerable bribe.

CHIC. The matter shall have my careful consideration. But my bride and her sisters approach, and any little compliment on your part, such as a politely abject grovel, would be esteemed a favor.

PRU. No money—no grovel!

(Exeunt together.)

(Enter procession of schoolgirls, with
TRILLIUM, PATTYCAKE, and PRISSY.)

CHORUS OF SCHOOLGIRLS

Comes a train of little ladies
> From scholastic trammels free.
Each a little bit afraid is,
> Wondering what the world can be!

Is it but a world of trouble—
    Sadness set to song?
Is its beauty but a bubble
    Bound to break ere long?

Are its palaces and pleasures
    Fantasies that fade?
And the glory of its treasures
    Shadow of a shade?

Schoolgirls we, eighteen and under,
    From scholastic trammels free,
And we wonder—how we wonder!
    What on earth the world can be!

TRIO—TRILLIUM, PATTYCAKE, and PRISSY

ALL 3. Three little maids from school are we,
Pert as a schoolgirl well can be,
Filled to the brim with girlish glee,
    Three little maids from school!
TRI. Everything is a source of fun.
PRI. Nobody's safe, for we care for none!
PAT.   Life is a joke that's just begun!
ALL 3.   Three little maids from school!
  Three little maids who, all unwary,
  Come from a ladies' seminary,
  Freed from its genius tutelary—
    Three little maids from school!

TRI.   One little maid is a bride, Trillium—
PRI.   Two little maids in attendance come—
PAT.   Three little maids is the total sum.
ALL 3.   Three little maids from school!
TRI.   From three little maids take one away.
PRI.   Two little maids remain, and they—
PAT.   Won't have to wait very long, they say—
ALL 3.   Three little maids from school!
  Three little maids who, all unwary,

Come from a ladies' seminary,
Freed from its genius tutelary—
    Three little maids from school!

(Enter CHICO and PRUFROCK.)

CHIC. At last, my bride that is to be! *(About to embrace her.)*
TRI. You're not going to kiss me before all these people?
CHIC. Well, that was the idea.
TRI. *(Aside to PRISSY.)* It seems odd, doesn't it?
PRI. It's rather peculiar.
PAT. Oh, I expect it's all right. Must have a beginning, you know.
TRI. Well, of course I know nothing about these things; but I've
    no objection if it's usual.
CHIC. Oh, it's quite usual, I think. Eh, Lord Chamberlain?
PRU. I have known it done. *(CHICO embraces TRILLIUM.)*
TRI. Thanks goodness that's over! *(Sees HANDY LOU.)* Why,
    that's never you? *(The **THREE GIRLS** rush to him and shake
    his hands, all speaking at once.)*
TRI. Oh, I'm so glad! I haven't seen you for ever so long, and
    I'm right at the top of the school, and I've got three prizes, and
    I've come home for good, and I'm not going back any more!
PRI. And have you got an engagement?—Trillium's got one, but
    she doesn't like it, and she'd ever so much rather it was you!
    I've come home for good, and I'm not going back any more!
PAT. Now tell us all the news, because you go about everywhere,
    and we've been at school, but, thank goodness, that's all over
    now, and we've come home for good, and we're not going
    back any more!

(The above three speeches spoken together in one breath.)

CHIC. I beg your pardon. Will you present me?

(ALL THREE speak at once.)

TRI. Oh, this is the musician who used—
PRI. Oh, this is the gentleman who used—
PAT. Oh, it is only Handy Lou who used—

CHIC. One at a time, if you please.

TRI. Oh, if you please, he's the gentleman who used to play so beautifully on the—on the—

PAT. On the Marine Parade.

TRI. Yes, I think that was the name of the instrument.

HAND. Sir, I have the misfortune to love your ward, Trillium— oh, I know I deserve your anger!

CHIC. Anger! Not a bit, my boy. Why, I love her myself. Charming little girl, isn't she? Pretty eyes, nice hair. Taking little thing, altogether. Very glad to hear my opinion backed by a competent authority. Thank you very much. Good-bye. *(To FACTOTUM.)* Take him away. *(FACTOTUM removes HANDY LOU.)*

PAT. *(Who has been examining PRUFROCK.)* I beg your pardon, but what is this?[5]

CHIC. That is a Tremendous Swell.

PAT. Oh, it's alive! *(Starts back in alarm.)*

PRU. Go away, little girls. Can't talk to little girls like you. Go away, there's dears.

CHIC. Allow me to present you, Lord Prufrock. These are my three wards. The one in the middle is my bride elect.

PRU. What do you want me to do to them? Mind, I will not kiss them.

CHIC. No, no, you shan't kiss them; a little bow—a mere nothing—you needn't mean it, you know.

PRU. It goes against the grain. They are not young ladies, they are young persons.

CHIC. Come, come, make an effort, there's a good nobleman.

PRU. Well, I shan't mean it. *(With a great effort.)* How de do, little girls, how de do? *(Aside.)* Oh, my protoplasmal ancestor!

CHIC. That's very good. *(GIRLS indulge in suppressed laughter.)*

PRU. I see nothing to laugh at. It is very painful to me to have to say "How de do, little girls, how de do?" to young persons. I'm not in the habit of saying "How de do, little girls, how de do?" to anybody under the rank of a Stockbroker.

CHIC. *(Aside to GIRLS.)* Don't laugh at him, he can't help it—

---

5   The phrase that traditionally follows "Customer come to try on?" looks to me like an idiom otherwise forgotten, at least in America.

he's under treatment for it. *(Aside to **PRUFROCK**.)* Never mind them, they don't understand the delicacy of your position.

PRU. We know how delicate it is, don't we?

CHIC. I should think we did! How a nobleman of your importance can do it at all is a thing I never can, never shall understand.

(CHICO retires up and goes off.)

QUARTET—TRILLIUM, PATTYCAKE, PRISSY, and PRUFROCK with CHORUS OF GIRLS

3 GIRLS. So please you, sir, we much regret
If we have failed in etiquette
Towards a man of rank so high—
We shall know better by and by.

TRI.   But youth, of course, must have its fling,
          So pardon us,
          So pardon us.

PAT.   And don't, in girlhood's happy spring,
          Be hard on us,
          Be hard on us,
If we're inclined to dance and sing.
          Tra la la, etc. *(Dancing.)*

ALL.   But youth, of course, etc.

PRU.   I think you ought to recollect
You cannot show too much respect
Towards the highly titled few;
But nobody does, and why should you?
That youth at us should have its fling,
          Is hard on us,
          Is hard on us;
To our prerogative we cling—
          So pardon us,
          So pardon us,
If we decline to dance and sing.
          Tra la la, etc. *(Dancing.)*

ALL.   But youth, of course, must have its fling, etc.

(Exeunt ALL but TRILLIUM.)

(Enter HANDY LOU.)

HAND. Trillium, at last we are alone! I have sought you night and day for three weeks, in the belief that your guardian was beheaded, and I find that you are about to be married to him this afternoon!

TRI. Alas, yes!

HAND. But you do not love him?

TRI. Alas, no!

HAND. Modified rapture! But why do you not refuse him?

TRI. What good would that do? He's my guardian, and he wouldn't let me marry you!

HAND. But I would wait until you were of age!

TRI. You forget that in Toboku girls do not arrive at years of discretion until they are fifty.

HAND. True; from seventeen to forty-nine are considered years of indiscretion.

TRI. Besides—a wandering minstrel, who plays a wind instrument outside teashops, is hardly a fitting husband for the ward of a Lord High Executioner.

HAND. But—*(Aside.)* Shall I tell her? Yes! She will not betray me! *(Aloud.)* What if it should prove that, after all, I am no musician?

TRI. There! I was certain of it, directly I heard you play!

HAND. What if it should prove that I am no other than the son of his Eminence the Grand Panjandrum?

TRI. The son of the Panjandrum! But why is your Excellency disguised? And what has your Excellency done? And will your Excellency promise never to do it again?

HAND. Some years ago I had the misfortune to captivate Nattyshaw, an elderly lady of my father's Court. She misconstrued my customary affability into expressions of affection, and claimed me in marriage, under my father's law. My father ordered me to marry her within a week, or perish ignominiously on the scaffold. That night I fled his Court, and, assuming the disguise of a Second Trombone, I joined the band in which you found me when I had the happiness of seeing you! *(Approaching her.)*

TRI. *(Retreating.)* If you please, I think your Excellency had better not come too near. The laws against flirting are excessively severe.

HAND. But we are quite alone, and nobody can see us.

TRI. Still, that doesn't make it right. To flirt is capital.

HAND. It *is* capital!

TRI. And we must obey the law.

HAND. Deuce take the law!

TRI. I wish it would, but it won't!

HAND. If it were not for that, how happy we might be!

TRI. Happy indeed!

HAND. If it were not for the law, we should now be sitting side by side, like that. *(Sits by her.)*

TRI. Instead of being obliged to sit half a mile off, like that. *(Crosses and sits at other side of stage.)*

HAND. We should be gazing into each other's eyes, like that. *(Gazing at her sentimentally.)*

TRI. Breathing sighs of unutterable love—like that. *(Sighing and gazing lovingly at him.)*

HAND. With our arms round each other's waists, like that. *(Embracing her.)*

TRI. Yes, if it wasn't for the law.

HAND. If it wasn't for the law.

TRI. As it is, of course we couldn't do anything of the kind.

HAND. Not for worlds!

TRI. Being engaged to Chico, you know!

HAND. Being engaged to Chico!

DUET—HANDY LOU and TRILLIUM

HAND.   Were you not to Chico plighted,
        I would say in tender tone,
   "Loved one, let us be united—
        Let us be each other's own!"
   I would merge all rank and station,

Worldly sneers are naught to us,
And, to mark my admiration,
I would kiss you fondly thus—*(Kisses her.)*
BOTH. {I, He} would kiss {you, me} fondly thus—*(Kiss.)*
TRI. But as I must marry elsewhere,
You and I must take a close care
No such hugs and kisses to share,
Lest ill luck should catch us up there![6]
Take care, take care, take care, take care!
HAND. So, in spite of all temptation,
Such a theme I'll not discuss,
And on no consideration
Will I kiss you fondly thus—*(Kisses her.)*
Let me make it clear to you,
This is what I'll never do!
This, oh, this, oh, this, oh, this—*(Kissing her.)*
BOTH. This, oh, this, etc.

(Exeunt in opposite directions.)

(Enter CHICO.)

CHIC. (Looking after **TRILLIUM**.) There she goes! To think how entirely my future happiness is wrapped up in that little parcel! Really, it hardly seems worth while! Oh, matrimony!—(Enter **PRU-FROCK** and **FACTOTUM**.) Now then, what is it? Can't you see I'm soliloquizing? You have interrupted an apostrophe, sirs!

FACT. I am the bearer of a letter from his Eminence the Panjandrum.

CHIC. (Taking it from him reverentially.) A letter from the Panjandrum! What in the world can he have to say to me? (Reads letter.) Ah, here it is at last! I thought it would come sooner or later! The Panjandrum is struck by the fact that no executions have taken place in the city for a year, and decrees that unless somebody is beheaded within one month, the post of Lord High Executioner shall be abol-

6   True, "yam for toko" isn't Japanese or mock-Japanese, as OED and other good dictionaries assure us—but it *sounds* like mock-Japanese, and how many people in the audience really read explanatory program notes? So I judged it best to find a substitute.

ished, and the city reduced to the rank of a village!

FACT. But that will involve us all in irretrievable ruin!

CHIC. Yes. There is no help for it, I shall have to execute somebody at once. The only question is, who shall it be?

PRU. Well, it seems unkind to say so, but as you're already under sentence of death for flirting, everything seems to point to you.

CHIC. To me? What are you talking about? I can't execute myself.

PRU. Why not?

CHIC. Why not? Because, in the first place, self-decapitation is an extremely difficult, not to say dangerous, thing to attempt; and, in the second it's suicide, and suicide is a capital offence.

PRU. That is so, no doubt.

FACT. We might reserve that point.

PRU. True, it could be argued six months hence, before the full Court.

CHIC. Besides, I don't see how a man can cut off his own head.

PRU. A man might try.

FACT. Even if you only succeeded in cutting it half off, that would be something.

PRU. It would be taken as an earnest of your desire to comply with the Panjandrumic will.

CHIC. No. Pardon me, but there I am adamant. As official Headsman, my reputation is at stake, and I can't consent to embark on a professional operation unless I see my way to a successful result.

PRU. This professional conscientiousness is highly creditable to you, but it places us in a very awkward position.

CHIC. My good sir, the awkwardness of your position is grace itself compared with that of a man engaged in the act of cutting off his own head.

FACT. I am afraid that, unless you can obtain a substitute—

CHIC. A substitute? Oh, certainly—nothing easier. (To ***PRU-FROCK***.) I appoint you Lord High Substitute.

PRU. I should be delighted. Such an appointment would realize my

TRIO—CHICO, PRUFROCK, and FACTOTUM

CHIC.   My brain it teems

With endless schemes
Both good and new
For Toboku;
But if I flit,
The benefit
That I'd diffuse
The town would lose!
Now every man
To aid his clan
Should plot and plan
As best he can,
    And so,
    Although
I'm ready to go,
Yet recollect
'Twere disrespect
Did I neglect
To thus effect
This aim direct,
So I object—

PRU.   I am so proud,
If I allowed
My family pride
To be my guide,
I'd volunteer
To quit this sphere
Instead of you,
In a minute or two.
But family pride
Must be denied,
And set aside,
And mortified.
    And so,
    Although
I wish to go,
And greatly pine
To brightly shine,
And take the line

Of a hero fine,
With grief condign,
I must decline—

FACT.   I heard one day
A gentleman say
That criminals who
Are cut in two
Can hardly feel
The fatal steel,
And so are slain
Without much pain.
If this is true,
It's jolly for you;
Your courage screw
To bid us adieu,
 And go
 And show
Both friend and foe
How much you dare.
I'm quite aware
It's your affair,
Yet I declare
I'd take your share,
But I don's much care—

ALL.   To sit in solemn silence in a dull, dark dock,
In a pestilential prison, with a lifelong lock,
Awaiting the sensation of a short, sharp shock,
From a cheap and chippy chopper on a big black block!

(Exeunt PRUFROCK and FACTOTUM.)

CHIC. This is simply appalling! I, who allowed myself to be re-
spited at the last moment, simply in order to benefit my native
town, am now required to die within a month, and that by a
man whom I have loaded with honors! Is this public grati-
tude? Is this—*(Enter HANDY LOU, with a rope in his hands.)*
Go away, sir! How dare you? Am I never to be permitted to

soliloquize?

HAND. Oh, go on—don't mind me.

CHIC. What are you going to do with that rope?

HAND. I am about to terminate an unendurable existence.

CHIC. Terminate your existence? Oh, nonsense! What for?

HAND. Because you are going to marry the girl I adore.

CHIC. Nonsense, sir. I won't permit it. I am a humane man, and if you attempt anything of the kind I shall order your instant arrest. Come, sir, desist at once, or I summon my guard.

HAND. That's absurd. If you attempt to raise an alarm, I instantly perform the Happy Dispatch with this dagger.

CHIC. No, no, don't do that. This is horrible! Why, you cold-blooded scoundrel, are you aware that, in taking your life, you are committing a crime which—which—which is—Oh! Substitute!

HAND. What's the matter?

CHIC. Is it *absolutely certain* that you are resolved to die?

HAND. Absolutely!

CHIC. Will *nothing* shake your resolution?

HAND. Nothing.

CHIC. Threats, entreaties, prayers—all useless?

HAND. All! My mind is made up.

CHIC. Then, if you really mean what you say, and if you are absolutely resolved to die, and if nothing whatever will shake your determination—don't spoil yourself by committing suicide, but be beheaded handsomely at the hands of the Lord High Executioner!

HAND. I don't see how that would benefit me.

CHIC. You don't? Observe: you'll have a month to live, and you'll live like a fighting-cock at my expense. When the day comes there'll be a grand public ceremonial—you'll be the central figure—no one will attempt to deprive you of that distinction. There'll be a procession—bands—dead march—bells tolling—all the girls in tears—Trillium distracted—then, when it's all over, general rejoicing, and a display of fireworks in the evening. *You* won't see them, but they'll be there all the same.

HAND. Do you think Trillium would really be distracted at my death?

CHIC. I am convinced of it. Bless you, she's the most tender-hearted little creature alive.

HAND. I should be sorry to cause her pain. Perhaps, after all, if I were to withdraw from Toboku, and travel the world for a couple of years, I might contrive to forget her.

CHIC. Oh, I don't think you could forget Trillium so easily; and, after all, what is more miserable than a love-blighted life?

HAND. True.

CHIC. Life without Trillium—why, it seems absurd!

HAND. And yet there are a good many people in the world who have to endure it.

CHIC. Poor devils, yes! You are quite right not to be of their number.

HAND. I *won't* be of their number!

CHIC. Noble fellow!

HAND. I'll tell you how we'll manage it. Let me marry Trillium tomorrow, and in a month you may behead me.

CHIC. No, no. I draw the line at Trillium.

HAND. Very good. If you can draw the line, so can I. *(Preparing rope.)*

CHIC. Stop, stop—listen one moment—be reasonable. How can I consent to your marring Trillium if I'm going to marry her myself?

HAND. My good friend, she'll be a widow in a month, and you can marry her then.

CHIC. That's true, of course. I quite see that. But, dear me! my position during the next month will be most unpleasant—most unpleasant.

HAND. Not half so unpleasant as my position at the end of it.

CHIC. But—dear me!—well—I agree—after all, it's only putting off my wedding for a month. But you won't prejudice her against me, will you? You see, I've educated her to be my wife; she's been taught to regard me as a wise and good man. Now I shouldn't like her views on that point disturbed.

HAND. Trust me, she shall never learn the truth from me.

FINALE

(Enter CHORUS, PRUFROCK, and FACTOTUM.)

CHOR.   With aspect stern
   And gloomy stride,
  We come to learn
   How you decide.
  Don't hesitate
   Your choice to name,
  A dreadful fate
   You'll suffer all the same.

PRU.   To ask you what you mean to do we punctually appear.
   CHIC.   Congratulate me, all of you, I've found a Volunteer!
   ALL.   Then let us raise a joyful noise of Hear, hear, hear!
CHIC. *(Presenting him.)* 'Tis Handy Lou!
ALL.   Hail, Handy Lou!
CHIC.   I think he'll do?
ALL.   Yes, yes, he'll do!
CHIC.   He yields his life if I Trillium surrender.
Now I adore that girl with passion tender,
And could not yield her with a ready will,
            Or her allot,
            If I did not
Adore myself with passion tenderer still!

(Enter TRILLIUM, PRISSY, and PATTYCAKE.)

ALL.   Ah, yes!
He loves himself with passion tenderer still!

CHIC. *(To HANDY LOU.)* Take her—she's yours!

(Exit CHICO.)

ENSEMBLE

HAND.   The threatened cloud has passed away,
TRIL.   And brightly shines the dawning day;
HAND.   What though the night may come too soon,
TRIL.   There's yet a month of afternoon!

HANDY LOU, PRUFROCK, FACTOTUM, TRILLIUM, PATTYCAKE, and PRISSY.

Then let the throng
    Our joy advance,
With laughing song
    And merry dance,
CHOR.   With joyous shout and ringing cheer,
Inaugurate {our, your} brief career!

PAT.   A day, a week, a month, a year—
TRI.   Or far or near, or far or near,
PRU.   Life's eventime comes much too soon,
PAT.   You'll live at least a honeymoon!
ALL.   Then let the throng, etc.
CHOR.   With joyous shout, etc.

SOLO—PRUFROCK

As in a month you've got to die,
    If Chico tells us true,
'Twere empty compliment to cry
    "Long life to Handy Lou!"
But as one month you have to live
    As fellow-citizen,
This toast with three times three we'll give—
    "Long life to you—till then!"

(Exit PRUFROCK.)

CHOR. May all good fortune prosper you,
May you have health and riches too,
May you succeed in all you do!
Long life to you—till then!

(Dance.)

(Enter NATTYSHAW melodramatically.)

NAT. Your revels cease! Assist me, all of you!
CHOR. Why, who is this whose evil eyes
Rain blight on our festivities?
NAT. I claim my perjured lover, Handy Lou!
Oh, fool! to shun delights that never cloy!
CHOR. Go, leave they deadly work undone!
NAT. Come back, oh, shallow fool! come back to joy!
CHOR. Away, away! ill-favored one!
HAND. *(Aside to TRILLIUM.)* Ah!
'Tis Nattyshaw!
The maid of whom I told you.   *(About to go.)*
NAT. *(Detaining him.)*   No!
You shall not go,
These arms shall thus enfold you!

SONG—NATTYSHAW

Oh fool, that fleest
  My hallowed joys!
Oh blind, that seest
  No equipoise!
Oh rash, that judgest
  From half, the whole!
Oh base, that grudgest
  Love's lightest dole!
      Thy heart unbind,
      Oh fool, oh blind!
      Give me my place,
      Oh rash, oh base!

CHOR.   If she's thy bride, restore her place,
Oh fool, oh blind, oh rash, oh base!

NAT. *(To **TRILLIUM**.)*
Pink cheek, that rulest
  Where wisdom serves!
Bright eye, that foolest
  Heroic nerves!
Rose lip, that scornest
  Love-laden years!
Smooth tongue, that warnest
  Who rightly hears!
      Thy doom is nigh,
      Pink cheek, bright eye!
      Thy knell is rung,
      Rose lip, smooth tongue!

CHOR.   If true her tale, thy knell is rung,
Pink cheek, bright eye, rose lip, smooth tongue!

PAT.   Away, nor prosecute your quest—
From our intention, well expressed,
      You cannot turn us!
The state of your connubial views
Towards the person you accuse
      Does not concern us!
For he's going to marry Trillium—
ALL.   Trillium!
PAT.   Your anger pray bury,
      For all will be merry,
I think you had better succumb—
ALL.   Cumb—cumb!
PAT.   And join our expressions of glee.
On this subject I pray you be dumb—
ALL.   Dumb—dumb.
PAT.   You'll find there are many
      Who'll wed for a penny—
The word for your guidance is "Mum"—

ALL.	Mum—mum!
PAT.	There's lots of good fish in the sea!
ALL.	On this subject we pray you be dumb, etc.

SOLO—NATTYSHAW

The hour of gladness
    Is dead and gone;
In silent sadness
    I live alone!
The hope I cherished
    All lifeless lies,
And all has perished
    Save love, which never dies!

Oh, faithless one, this insult you shall rue!
In vain for mercy on your knees you'll sue.
    I'll tear the mask from your disguising!

HAND. *(Aside.)*	Now comes the blow!
NAT.	Prepare yourselves for news surprising!
HAND. *(Aside.)*	How foil my foe?
NAT.	No minstrel he, despite his thrum-thrum!
TRI. *(Aside.)*	Ha! ha! I know!
NAT.	He is the son of your—

(HANDY LOU, TRILLIUM, and CHORUS,
interrupting to drown her voice.)

	O my! Pobble without any tum-tum!
NAT.	In vain with noise you seek to overcome!
	He is the only son of your—
ALL.	O my! Pobble without any tum-tum!
NAT.	I'll spoil—
ALL.	O my! Pobble without any tum-tum!
NAT.	Your loud bru-brum-brum!
	He is the son—
ALL.	O my! Pobble without any

tum-tum!

NAT.   Of your—

ALL.   O my! Pobble without any tum-tum!

NAT.   The son of your—

ALL.   O my! Pobble without any
tum-tum! O my! O my!

ENSEMBLE

NATTYSHAW.   Ye torrents roar!
Ye tempests howl!
Your wrath outpour
With angry growl!
Do ye your worst, my vengeance call
Shall rise triumphant over all!
Prepare for woe,
Ye haughty lords,
At once I go
Panjandrum-wards.
My wrongs with vengeance shall be crowned!
My wrongs with vengeance shall be crowned!

THE OTHERS.   We'll hear no more,
Ill-omened owl,
To joy we soar,
Despite your scowl!
The echoes of our festival
Shall rise triumphant over all!
Away you go,
Collect your hordes;
Proclaim your woe
In dismal chords;
We do not heed their dismal sound,
For joy reigns everywhere around.

*(NATTYSHAW rushes furiously upstage, clearing the crowd
away right and left, finishing on steps at back of stage.)*

END OF ACT I

ACT II

SOLO - PATTYCAKE with CHORUS

CHOR.   Braid the raven *[golden, auburn, russet, etc.]* hair—
   Weave the supple tress—
Deck the maiden fair
   In her loveliness—
Paint the pretty face—
   Dye the coral lip—
Emphasize the grace
   Of her ladyship!
Art and nature, thus allied,
Go to make a pretty bride.

PAT.   Sit with downcast eye—
   Let it brim with dew—
Try if you can cry—
   We will do so, too.
When you're summoned, start
   Like a frightened roe—
Flutter, little heart,
   Color, come and go!
Modesty at marriage-tide
Well becomes a pretty bride!

CHOR. Braid the raven *[or whatever color]* hair, etc.

(Exeunt ALL but TRILLIUM.)

TRIL. Yes, I am indeed beautiful! Sometimes I sit and wonder, in my artless maidenly way, why it is that I am so much more attractive than anybody else in the whole world. Can this be vanity? No! Nature is lovely and rejoices in her loveliness. I am a child of Nature, and take after my mother.

SONG—TRILLIUM

The sun, whose rays
Are all ablaze
   With ever-living glory,
Does not deny
His majesty—
   He scorns to tell a story.
He don't exclaim,
"I blush for shame,
   So kindly be indulgent."
But, fierce and bold,
In fiery gold
   He glories all effulgent!

          I mean to rule the earth,
            As he the sky—
          We really know our worth,
            The sun and I!

Observe his flame,
That placid dame,
   The moon's Celestial Highness;
There's not a trace
Upon her face
   Of diffidence or shyness:
She borrows light
That, through the night,
   The world[7] may all acclaim her!
And, truth to tell,
She lights up well,
   So I, for one, don't blame her!

---

[7]   Where quite convenient, I prefer gender-inclusive language.

Ah, pray make no mistake,
  We are not shy;
We're very wide awake,
  The moon and I!

(Enter PATTYCAKE and PRISSY.)

TRI. Yes, everything seems to smile upon me. I am to be married today to the man I love best, and I believe I am the very happiest girl in Toboku!

PRI. The happiest girl indeed, for she is indeed to be envied who has attained happiness in all but perfection.

TRI. In "all but" perfection?

PRI. Well, dear, it can't be denied that the fact that your husband is to be beheaded in a month is, in its way, a drawback. It does seem to take the top off it, you know.

PAT. I don't know about that. It all depends!

PRI. At all events, *he* will find it a drawback!

PAT. Not necessarily. Bless you, it all depends!

TRI. *(In tears.)* I think it very indelicate of you to refer to such a subject on such a day. If my married happiness *is* to be—to be—

PRI. Cut short.

TRI. Well, cut short—in a month, can't you let me forget it? *(Weeping.)*

(Enter HANDY LOU, followed by FACTOTUM.)

HAND. Trillium in tears—and on her wedding morn!

TRI. They've been reminding me that in a month you're to be beheaded! *(Weeps.)*

PAT. Yes, we've been reminding her that you're to be beheaded. *(Bursts into tears.)*

PRI. It's quite true, you know, you *are* going to be beheaded! *(Bursts into tears.)*

HAND. *(Aside.)* Humph! Now, some bridegrooms would be depressed by this sort of thing! *(Aloud.)* A month? Well, what's a month? Bah! These divisions of time are purely arbitrary. Who says twenty-four hours make a day?

PAT. There's a popular impression to that effect.

HAND. Then we'll efface it. We'll call each second a minute—each minute an hour—each hour a day—and each day a year. At that rate we've about thirty years of married happiness before us!

PRI. And, at that rate, this interview has already lasted four hours and three-quarters! *(Exit PRISSY.)*

TRI. Yes. How time flies when one is thoroughly enjoying oneself!

HAND. That's the way to look at it! Don't let's be downhearted! There's a silver lining to every cloud.

TRI. Certainly. Let's—let's be perfectly happy!

FACT. By all means. Let's—let's thoroughly enjoy ourselves.

PAT. It's—it's absurd to cry!

TRI. Quite ridiculous!

(ALL break into a forced and melancholy laugh.)

MADRIGAL—TRILLIUM, PATTYCAKE, HANDY LOU, and FACTOTUM

Brightly dawns our wedding day;
> Joyous hour, we give thee greeting!
> Whither, whither art thou fleeting?
Fickle moment, prithee stay!
> What though mortal joys be hollow?
> Pleasures come, if sorrows follow:
Though the tocsin sound ere long,
> Ding dong! Ding dong!
Yet until the shadows fall
Over one and over all,
Sing a merry madrigal—
Fal-la—fal-la! etc.

Let us dry the ready tear,
> Though the hours are surely creeping
> Little need for woeful weeping,
Till the sad sundown is near.

All must sip the cup of sorrow—
I today and thou tomorrow;
This the close of every song—
Ding dong! Ding dong!
What though solemn shadows fall,
Sooner, later, over all?
Sing a merry madrigal—
Fal-la—fal-la! etc. *(Ending in tears.)*

(Exeunt PATTYCAKE and FACTOTUM.)

**(HANDY LOU embraces TRILLIUM. Enter
CHICO. HANDY LOU releases TRILLIUM.)**

CHIC. Go on—don't mind me.

HAND. I'm afraid we're distressing you.

CHIC. Never mind, I must get used to it. Only please do it by degrees. Begin by putting your arm round her waist. *(HANDY LOU does so.)* There; let me get used to that first.

TRI. Oh, wouldn't you like to retire? It must pain you to see us so affectionate together!

CHIC. No. I must learn to bear it! Now oblige me by allowing her head to rest on your shoulder.

HAND. Like that?

CHIC. I am much obliged to you. Now—kiss her! *(HANDY LOU does so. CHICO writhes with anguish.)* Thank you—it's simple torture!

TRI. Come, come, bear up! After all, it's only for a month.

CHIC. No. It's no use deluding oneself with false hopes.

HAND. & TRI. What do you mean?

CHIC. *(To TRILLIUM.)* My child—my poor child! *(Aside.)* How shall I break it to her? *(Aloud.)* My little bride that was to have been—

TRI. *(Delighted.) Was* to have been?

CHIC. Yes, you never can be mine!

HAND. What?

TRI. I'm so glad! *(They speak together in ecstasy.)*

CHIC. I've just ascertained that, by the Panjandrum's law, when a married man is beheaded his wife is buried alive.

HAND. & TRI. Buried alive!

CHIC. Buried alive. It's a most unpleasant death.

HAND. But whom did you get that from?

CHIC. Oh, from Lord Prufrock. He's my Solicitor.

TRI. But he may be mistaken!

CHIC. So I thought; so I consulted the Attorney-General, the Lord Chief Justice, the Master of the Rolls, the Judge Ordinary, and the Lord Chancellor. They're all of the same opinion. Never knew such unanimity on a point of law in my life!

HAND. But stop a bit! This law has never been put in force.

CHIC. Not yet. You see, flirting is the only crime punishable with decapitation, and married men never flirt.

HAND. Of course they don't. I quite forgot that! Well, I suppose I may take it that my dream of happiness is at an end!

TRI. Darling—I don't want to appear selfish, and I love you with all my heart—I don't suppose I shall ever love anybody else half as much—but when I agreed to marry you—my own—I had no idea—pet—that I should have to be buried alive in a month!

HAND. Nor I! It's the very first I've heard of it!

TRI. It—makes a difference, doesn't it?

HAND. It *does* make a difference, of course.

TRI. You see—burial alive—it's such a stuffy death!

HAND. I call it a beast of a death.

TRI. You see my difficulty, don't you?

HAND. Yes, and I see my own. If I insist on your carrying out your promise, I doom you to a hideous death; if I release you, you marry Chico at once!

TRIO—TRILLIUM, HANDY LOU, and CHICO

TRI.   Here's a how-de-do!
If I marry you,
When your time has come to perish,
Then the maiden whom you cherish
    Must be slaughtered, too!
    Here's a how-de-do!

HAND.   Here's a pretty mess!
    In a month, or less,

I must die without a wedding!
Let the bitter tears I'm shedding
    Witness my distress,
    Here's a pretty mess!

CHIC.   Here's a state of things!
    To her life she clings!
Matrimonial devotion
Doesn't seem to suit her notion—
    Burial it brings!
    Here's a state of things!

ALL.   With a passion that's intense
              {I, You} worship and adore,
But the laws of common sense
              {We, You} oughtn't to ignore.
If what {he,I} say{s} is true,
              'Tis death to marry you!
Here's a pretty state of things!
              Here's a pretty how-de-do!

(Exit TRILLIUM.)

CHIC. My poor boy, I'm really very sorry for you.

HAND. Thanks, old fellow. I'm sure you are.

CHIC. You see I'm quite helpless.

HAND. I quite see that.

CHIC. I can't conceive anything more distressing that to have one's marriage broken off at the last moment. But you shan't be disappointed of a wedding—you shall come to mine.

HAND. It's awfully kind of you, but that's impossible.

CHIC. Why so?

HAND. Today I die.

CHIC. What do you mean?

HAND. I can't live without Trillium. This afternoon I perform the Happy Dispatch.

CHIC. No, no—pardon me—I can't allow that.

HAND. Why not?

CHIC. Why, hang it all, you're under contract to die by the hand of the Lord High Executioner in a month's time! If you kill yourself, what's to become of me? Why, I shall have to be executed in your place!

HAND. It would certainly seem so.

(Enter PRUFROCK.)

CHIC. Now then, Lord Mayor, what is it?

PRU. The Panjandrum and his suite are approaching the city, and will be here in ten minutes.

CHIC. The Panjandrum! He's coming to see whether his orders have been carried out! *(To HANDY LOU.)* Now look here, you know—this is getting serious—a bargain's a bargain, and you really mustn't frustrate the ends of justice by committing suicide. As a man of honor and a gentleman, you are bound to die ignominiously by the hands of the Lord High Executioner.

HAND. Very well, then—behead me.

CHIC. What, now?

HAND. Certainly; at once.

PRU. Chop it off, Chico, chop it off!

CHIC. My good sir, I don't go about prepared to execute gentlemen at a moment's notice. Why, I never even killed a bluebottle fly!

PRU. Still, as Lord High Executioner—

CHIC. My good sir, as Lord High Executioner, I've got to behead him in a month. I'm not ready yet. I don't know how it's done. I'm going to take lessons. I mean to begin with a guinea pig, and work my way through the animal kingdom till I come to a Second Trombone. Why, you don't suppose that, as a humane man, I'd have accepted the post of Lord High Executioner if I hadn't thought the duties were purely nominal? I *can't* kill you—I can't kill anything! I can't kill anybody! *(Weeps.)*

HAND. Come, my poor fellow, we all have unpleasant duties to discharge at times; after all, what is it? If I don't mind, why should you? Remember, sooner or later it must be done.

CHIC. *(Springing up suddenly.)* Must it? I'm not so sure about that!

HAND. What do you mean?

CHIC. Why should I kill you when making an affidavit that you've been executed will do just as well? Here are plenty of witnesses—the Lord Chief Justice, Lord High Admiral, Commander-in-Chief, Secretary of State for the Home Department, First Lord of the Treasury, and Chief Commissioner of Police.

HAND. But where are they?

CHIC. There they are. They'll all swear to it—won't you?

PRU. Am I to understand that all of us high Officers of State are required to perjure ourselves to ensure your safety?

CHIC. Why not? You'll be grossly insulted, as usual.

PRU. Will the insult be cash down, or at a date?

CHIC. It will be a ready-money transaction.

PRU. Well, it will be a useful discipline. Very good. Choose your fiction, and I'll endorse it! *(Aside.)* Ha! ha! Family Pride, how do you like *that,* my buck?

HAND. But I tell you that life without Trillium—

CHIC. Oh, Trillium, Trillium! Bother Trillium! Here, Commissioner, go and fetch Trillium. *(Exit PRUFROCK.)* Take Trillium and marry Trillium, only go away and never come back again. *(Enter PRUFROCK with TRILLIUM.)* Here she is. Trillium, are you particularly busy?

TRI. Not particularly.

CHIC. You've five minutes to spare?

TRI. Yes.

CHIC. Then go along with his Grace the Archbishop of Toboku; he'll marry you at once.

TRI. But if I'm to be buried alive?

CHIC. Now, don't ask any questions, but do as I tell you, and Handy Lou will explain all.

HAND. But one moment—

CHIC. Not for worlds. Here comes the Panjandrum, no doubt to ascertain whether I've obeyed his decree, and if he finds you alive I shall have the greatest difficulty in persuading him that I've beheaded you. *(Exeunt HANDY LOU and TRILLIUM, followed by PRUFROCK.)* Close thing that, for here he comes! *(Exit CHICO.)*

(March—Enter procession, heralding
PANJANDRUM, with NATTYSHAW.)

MARCH *(from "Iolanthe"—use as much as desired.)*

CHOR.   Loudly let the trumpet bray!
　　　　　　Tantantara!
　　Proudly bang the sounding brasses!
　　　　　　Tzing! Boom!
　As upon his lordly way
　　Our unique Panjandrum passes,
　　　　　Tantantara! Tzing! Boom!
　Bow, bow, ye lower middle classes!
　Bow, bow, ye tradesman, bow, ye masses!
　Blow the trumpets, bang the brasses!
　　　　　Tantantara! Tzing! Boom!
　He is lord of highest station,
　Paragon of legislation,
　Keystone of our mighty nation!
　　　　　Tantantara! Tzing! Boom!

DUET—PANJANDRUM and NATTYSHAW

PAN.　　　　　From every kind of man
　　Obedience I expect;
　I am the mighty Pan—
NAT.　　　　　　And I'm his daughter-in-law elect!
　　He'll marry his son
　　(He's only got one)
　To his daughter-in-law elect!
PAN.　　　　　My morals have been declared
　　Particularly correct;
NAT.　　　　　　But they're nothing at all, compared
　With those of his daughter-in-law elect!
　　　　Bow—Bow—
　To his daughter-in-law elect.

PAN.　　　　　In a fatherly kind of way
　　I govern each tribe and sect,
　All cheerfully own my sway—
NAT.　　　　　　Except his daughter-in-law elect!
　　As tough as a bone,
　　With a will of her own,
　Is his daughter-in-law elect!

PAN.   My nature is love and light—
    My freedom from all defect—
NAT.   Is insignificant quite,
    Compared with his daughter-in-law elect!
        Bow—Bow—
    To his daughter-in-law elect!
ALL.   Bow—Bow—
    To his daughter-in-law elect!

SONG—PANJANDRUM with CHORUS

PAN.   A ruler more humane did ne'er
    In Toboku exist.
        To nobody second,
        I'm certainly reckoned
    A true philanthropist.
  It is my very humane endeavor
    To make, to some extent,
        Each evil liver
        A running river
  Of harmless merriment.

        My object all sublime
        I shall achieve in time—
  To let the punishment fit the crime—
          The punishment fit the crime;
        And make each prisoner pent
        Unwillingly represent
  A source of innocent merriment!
        Of innocent merriment!

All prosy dull society sinners,
  Who chatter and bleat and bore,
    Are sent to hear sermons
    From mystical Germans
  Who preach from ten till four.
The amateur tenor, whose vocal villainies
  All desire to shirk,
    Shall, during off-hours,
    Exhibit his powers

To Madame Tussaud's waxwork.

The person who platitudes every disaster
   With words that what *is,* must be right,
      And 'twill have a good end,
      That numskull we send
   To sleep in a morgue every night.[8]
The idiot who, in railway carriages,
   Scribbles on window-panes,
      We only suffer
      To ride on a buffer
  In Parliamentary trains.

      My object all sublime, etc.

CHOR.   His object all sublime, etc.

PAN.   The advertising quack who wearies
  With tales of countless cures,
     His teeth, I've enacted,
     Shall all be extracted
  By terrified amateurs.
The music-hall singer attends a series
  Of masses and fugues and 'ops'
     By Bach, interwoven
     With Spohr and Beethoven,
  At classical Monday Pops.

The billiard sharp whom anyone catches,
  His doom's extremely hard—
     He's made to dwell
     In a dungeon cell
  On a spot that's always barred.
And there he plays extravagant matches
    In fitless finger-stalls

---

8   Whatever I have ever heard or can imagine done with the lines about "the lady who dyes a chemical yellow,", it remains racist —after all, the lady's punishment is to be dyed black!—with strong overtones of sexism, ageism, and lookism thrown in for good measure. Overly optimistic Pangloss types can be either gender and any age.

On a cloth untrue,
With a twisted cue
And elliptical billiard balls!

My object all sublime, etc.

CHOR.   His object all sublime, etc.

(Enter PRUFROCK, CHICO, and PATTYCAKE, who all kneel. PRUFROCK hands a paper to CHICO.)

CHIC. I am honored in being permitted to welcome your Eminence. I guessed the object of your Eminence's visit—your wishes have been attended to. The execution has taken place.

PAN. Oh, you've had an execution, have you?

CHIC. Yes. The Coroner has just handed me his certificate.

PRU. I am the Coroner. *(CHICO hands certificate to PANJANDRUM.)*

PAN. And this is the certificate of his death. *(Reads.)* "Here in our city, in the presence of the Lord Chancellor, Lord Chief Justice, Attorney-General, Secretary of State for the Home Department, Lord Mayor, and Groom of the Second Floor Front—"

PRU. They were all present, your Eminence. I counted them myself.

PAN. Very good house. I wish I'd been in time for the performance.

CHIC. A tough fellow he was, too—a man of gigantic strength. His struggles were terrific. It was really a remarkable scene.

PAN. Describe it.

TRIO—CHICO, PATTYCAKE, and PRUFROCK, with CHORUS

CHIC.   The criminal cried, as he dropped him down,
In a state of wild alarm—
With a frightful, frantic, fearful frown,
I bared my big right arm.
I seized him by the scruff of his neck,
And on his knees fell he,
As he squirmed and struggled,

And gurgled and guggled,
I drew my snickersnee!
    Oh, never shall I
    Forget the cry,
Or the shriek that shriek-ed he,
    As I gnashed my teeth,
    When from its sheath
I drew my snickersnee!

CHOR.   We know him well,
    He cannot tell
Untrue or groundless tales—
    He always tries
    To utter lies,
And every time he fails.

PAT.   He shivered and shook as he gave the sign
  For the stroke he didn't deserve;
When all of a sudden his eye met mine,
  And it seemed to brace his nerve;
For he nodded his head and kissed his hand,
  And he whistled an air, did he,
    As the saber true
    Cut cleanly through
His cervical vertebrae!
    When a man's afraid,
    A beautiful maid
Is a cheering sight to see;
    And it's oh, I'm glad
    That moment sad
Was soothed by sight of me!

CHOR.   Her terrible tale
    You can't assail,
With truth it quite agrees:
    Her taste exact
    For faultless fact
Amounts to a disease.

PRU.   Now though you'd have said that head was dead
   (For its owner dead was he),
It stood on its neck, with a smile well-bred,
   And bowed three times to me!
It was none of your impudent off-hand nods,
   But as humble as could be;
      For it clearly knew
      The deference due
   To a man of pedigree!
      And it's oh, I vow,
      This deathly bow
   Was a touching sight to see;
      Though trunkless, yet
      It couldn't forget
   The deference due to me!

CHOR.   This haughty youth,
   He speaks the truth
Whenever he finds it pays:
   And in this case
   It all took place
Exactly as he says!

(Exeunt CHORUS.)

PAN. All this is very interesting, and I should like to have seen it. But we came about a totally different matter. A year ago my son, the heir to the throne of Toboku, bolted from our Panjan-drumic Court.

CHIC. Indeed! Had he any reason to be dissatisfied with his position?

NAT. None whatever. On the contrary, I was going to marry him—yet he fled!

PRU. I am surprised that he should have fled from one so lovely!

NAT. That's not true—you are not surprised.

PRU. No!

NAT. You hold that I am not beautiful because my face is plain. But you know nothing: you are still unenlightened. Learn, then, that it is not in the face alone that beauty is to be sought.

My face is unattractive!

PRU. It is.

NAT. But I have a left shoulder-blade that is a miracle of loveliness. People come miles to see it. My right elbow has a fascination that few can resist.

PRU. Allow me!

NAT. It is on view Tuesdays and Fridays, on presentation of visiting card. As for my circulation, it is the largest in the world.

CHIC. And yet he fled!

PAN. And is now masquerading in this town, disguised as a Second Trombone.

CHIC., PRU., and **PAT.** *(Speaking together.)* A Second Trombone!

PAN. Yes; would it be troubling you too much if I asked you to produce him? He goes by the name of—

NAT. Handy Lou.

PAN. Handy Lou.

CHIC. It's quite easy. That is, it's rather difficult. In point of fact, he's gone abroad!

PAN. Gone abroad! His address.

CHIC. Barataria![9]

NAT. *(Reading death certificate.)* Ha!

PAN. What's the matter?

NAT. See here—his name—Handy Lou—beheaded this morning. Oh, where shall I find another? Where shall I find another?

*(**CHICO, PRUFROCK,** and **PATTYCAKE** fall on their knees.)*

PAN. *(Looking at certificate.)* Dear, dear, dear! this is very tiresome. *(To **CHICO**.)* My poor fellow, in your anxiety to carry out my wishes you have beheaded the heir to the throne of Toboku!

CHIC. I beg to offer an unqualified apology.

PRU. I desire to associate myself with that expression of regret.

PAT. We really hadn't the least notion—

PAN. Of course you hadn't. How could you? Come, come, my

---

9   Knightsbridge, the site Ko-Ko names in the original libretto, was the scene of an influential "Japanese village" when Gilbert wrote *The Mikado*—though no one is very likely to remember that allusion today; and in any case it's become traditional to name a local or currently notable place.

good fellow, don't distress yourself—it was no fault of yours. If a man of exalted rank chooses to disguise himself as a Second Trombone, he must take the consequences. It really distresses me to see you take on so. I've no doubt he thoroughly deserved all he got. *(They rise.)*

CHIC. We are infinitely obliged to your Eminence—

PAT. Much obliged, your Eminence.

PRU. Very much obliged, your Eminence.

PAN. Obliged? Not a bit. Don't mention it. How *could* you tell?

PRU. No, of course we couldn't tell who the gentleman really was.

PAT. It wasn't written on his forehead, you know.

CHIC. It might have been on his calling card; but Second Trombones don't carry calling cards! Ha! ha! ha!

PAN. Ha! ha! ha! *(To NATTYSHAW.)* I forget the punishment for compassing the death of the Heir Apparent.

CHIC., PRU., and **PAT.** *(Together; dropping down on their knees again.)* Punishment!

PAN. Yes. Something lingering, with boiling oil in it, I fancy. Something of that sort. I think boiling oil occurs in it, but I'm not sure. I know it's something humorous, but lingering, with either boiling oil or melted lead. Come, come, don't fret—I'm not a bit angry.

CHIC. If your Eminence will accept our assurance, we had no idea—

PAN. Of course—

PAT. I knew nothing about it.

PRU. I wasn't there.

PAN. That's the pathetic part of it. Unfortunately, the fool of an Act says "compassing the death of the Heir Apparent." There's not a word about a mistake—

CHIC., PRU., and **PAT.** No!

PAN. Or not knowing—

CHIC. No!

PAN. Or having no notion—

PAT. No!

PAN. Or not being there—

PRU. No!

PAN. There should be, of course—

CHIC., PRU., and **PAT.** Yes!

PAN. But there isn't.

CHIC., PRU., and **PAT.** Oh!

PAN. That's the slovenly way in which these Acts are always drawn. However, cheer up, it'll be all right. I'll have it altered next session. Now, let's see about your execution—will after luncheon suit you? Can you wait till then?

CHIC., PRU., and **PAT.** Oh, yes—we can wait till then!

PAN. Then we'll make it after luncheon.

PRU. I don't want any lunch.

PAN. I'm really very sorry for you all, but it's an unjust world, and virtue is triumphant only in theatrical performances.

GLEE—the FIVE

PAN.
    See how the Fates their gifts allot,
  For A is happy—B is not.
  Yet Be is worthy, I dare say,
  Of more prosperity than A!

CH., PR., & PAT.   *Is* B more worthy?

NAT.   I should say
  He's worth a great deal more than A.

ALL.   Yet A is happy!
    Oh, so happy!
   Laughing, Ha! ha!
   Chaffing, Ha! ha!
  Nectar quaffing, Ha! ha! ha!
   Ever joyous, ever gay,
   Happy, undeserving A!

CH., PR., & PAT.   If I were Fortune—which I'm not—
  B should enjoy A's happy lot,
  And A should die in miserie—
  That is, assuming I am B.

PAN. & NAT.   But *should* A perish?

CH., PR., & PAT.   That should he
  (Of course, assuming I am B).
   B should be happy!
    Oh, so happy!
   Laughing, Ha! ha!

Chaffing, Ha! ha!
Nectar quaffing, Ha! ha! ha!
But condemned to die is he,
Wretched meritorious B!

(Exeunt PANJANDRUM and NATTYSHAW.)

CHIC. Well, a nice mess you've got us into, with your nodding head and the deference due to a man of pedigree!

PRU. Merely corroborative detail, intended to give artistic verisimilitude to an otherwise bald and unconvincing narrative.

PAT. Corroborative detail indeed! Corroborative fiddlestick!

CHIC. And you're just as bad as he is, with your cock-and-bull stories about catching his eye and his whistling an air. But that's so like you! You must put in your oar!

PRU. But how about your big right arm?

PAT. Yes, and your snickersnee!

CHIC. Well, well, never mind that now. There's only one thing to be done. Handy Lou hasn't started yet—he must come to life again at once. *(Enter HANDY LOU and TRILLIUM.)* Here he comes. Here, Handy Lou, I've good news for you—you're reprieved.

HAND. Oh, but it's too late. I'm a dead man, and I'm off for my honeymoon.

CHIC. Nonsense! A terrible thing has just happened. It seems you're the son of the Panjandrum.

HAND. Yes, but that happened some time ago.

CHIC. Is this a time for airy persiflage? Your father is here, and with Nattyshaw.

HAND. My father! And with Nattyshaw!

CHIC. Yes, he wants you particularly.

PRU. So does she.

TRI. Oh, but he's married now.

CHIC. But, bless my heart! what has that to do with it?

HAND. Nattyshaw claims me in marriage, but I can't marry her because I'm married already—consequently she will insist on my execution, and if I'm executed, my wife will have to be buried alive.

TRI. You see our difficulty.

CHIC. Yes. I don't know what's to be done.

HAND. There's one chance for you. If you could persuade Nattyshaw to marry you, she would have no further claim on me, and in that case I could come to life without any fear of being put to death.

CHIC. I marry Nattyshaw!

TRI. I really think it's the only course.

CHIC. But, my good girl, have you seen her? She's something appalling!

PAT. Ah! that's only her face. She has a left elbow which people come miles to see!

PRU. I am told that her right heel is much admired by connoisseurs.

CHIC. My good sir, I decline to pin my heart upon any lady's right heel.

HAND. It comes to this: While Nattyshaw is single, I prefer to be a disembodied spirit. When Nattyshaw is married, existence will be as welcome as the flowers in spring.

DUET—HANDY LOU and CHICO with TRILLIUM, PATTYCAKE, and PRUFROCK

HAND.   The flowers that bloom in the spring,
            Tra la,
    Breathe promise of merry sunshine—
As we merrily dance and we sing,
            Tra la,
We welcome the hope that they bring,
            Tra la,
Of a summer of roses and wine.
    And that's what we mean when we say that a thing
Is welcome as flowers that bloom in the spring.
            Tra la la la la la, etc.

ALL.   Tra la la la, etc.

CHIC.   The flowers that bloom in the spring,
            Tra la,
    Have nothing to do with the case.
I've got to take under my wing,

Tra la,
A most unattractive old thing,
Tra la,
With a caricature of a face,
And that's what I mean when I say or I sing,
"Oh, bother the flowers that bloom in the spring."
Tra la la la la la, etc.

ALL.   Tra la la la, etc.

(Dance and exeunt ALL.)

(Enter NATTYSHAW.)

RECITATIVE and SONG—NATTYSHAW

Alone, and yet alive! Oh, sepulcher!
My soul is still my body's prisoner!
Remote the peace that Death alone can give—
My doom, to wait! my punishment, to live!

Hearts do not break!
They sting and ache
For old love's sake,
        But do not die.
Though with each breath
They long for death
As witnesseth
        The living I!
                Oh, living I!
                Come, tell me why,
                When hope is gone,
                Dost thou stay on?
                Why linger here,
                Where all is drear?
                Oh, living I!
                Come, tell me why,
                When hope is gone,

Dost thou stay on?
May not a cheated maiden die?

CHIC. *(Entering and approaching her timidly.)* Nattyshaw!

NAT. The miscreant who robbed me of my love! But vengeance pursues—they are heating the cauldron!

CHIC. Nattyshaw—behold a suppliant at your feet! Nattyshaw—mercy!

NAT. Mercy? Had you mercy on him? See here, you! You have slain my love. He did not love *me,* but he would have loved me in time. I am an acquired taste—only the educated palate can appreciate *me.* I was educating *his* palate when he left me. Well, he is dead, and where shall I find another? It takes years to train a man to love me. Am I to go through the weary round again, and, at the same time, implore mercy for you who robbed me of my prey—I mean my pupil—just as his education was on the point of completion? Oh, where shall I find another?

CHIC. Here!—Here!

NAT. What!!!

CHIC. Nattyshaw, for years I have loved you with a white-hot passion that is slowly but surely consuming my very vitals! Ah, shrink not from me! If there is aught of woman's mercy in your heart, turn not away from a lovesick suppliant whose every fiber thrills at your tiniest touch! True it is that, under a poor mask of disgust, I have endeavored to conceal a passion whose inner fires are broiling the soul within me! But the fire will not be smothered—it defies all attempts at extinction, and, breaking forth all the more eagerly for its long restraint, it declares itself in words that will not be weighed—that cannot be schooled—that should not be too severely criticized. Nattyshaw, I dare not hope for your love—but I will not live without it!

NAT. You, whose hands still reek with the blood of my betrothed, dare to address words of passion to the woman you have so foully wronged!

CHIC. I do—accept my love, or I perish on the spot!

NAT. Go to! Who knows so well as I that no one ever yet died of a broken heart!

CHIC. You know not what you say. Listen!

SONG—CHICO

On a tree by a river a little tom-tit
    Sang "Willow, titwillow, titwillow!"
And I said to him, "Dicky-bird, why do you sit
    Singing 'Willow, titwillow, titwillow'?
Is it weakness of intellect, birdie?" I cried,
"Or a rather tough worm in your little inside?"
With a shake of his poor little head, he replied,
    "Oh, willow, titwillow, titwillow!"

He slapped at his chest, as he sat on that bough,
    Singing "Willow, titwillow, titwillow!"
And a cold perspiration bespangled his brow,
    "Oh, willow, titwillow, titwillow!"
He sobbed and he sighed, and a gurgle he gave,
Then he plunged himself into the billowy wave,
And an echo arose from the suicide's grave—
    "Oh, willow, titwillow, titwillow!"

Now I feel just as sure as I'm sure that my name
    Isn't Willow, titwillow, titwillow,
That 'twas blighted affection that made him exclaim,
    "Oh, willow, titwillow, titwillow!"
And if you remain callous and obdurate, I
Shall perish as he did, and you will know why,
Though I probably shall not exclaim as I die,
    "Oh, willow, titwillow, titwillow!"

*(During this song NATTYSHAW has been greatly
affected, and at the end is almost in tears.)*

NAT. Did he really die of love?
CHIC. He really did.
NAT. All on account of a cruel little hen?
CHIC. Yes.
NAT. Poor little chap!
CHIC. It's an affecting tale, and quite true. I knew the bird inti-

mately.

NAT. Did you? He must have been very fond of her.

CHIC. His devotion was something extraordinary.

NAT. Poor little chap! And—and if I refuse you, will you go and do the same?

CHIC. At once.

NAT. No, no—you mustn't! Anything but that! *(Falls on his breast.)* Oh, I'm a silly little goose!

CHIC. You are!

NAT. And you won't hate me because I'm just a little teeny weeny wee bit bloodthirsty, will you?

CHIC. Hate you? Oh, Nattyshaw! is there not beauty even in bloodthirstiness?

NAT. My idea exactly.

DUET—CHICO and NATTYSHAW

NAT.
There is beauty in the bellow of the blast,
There is grandeur in the growling of the gale,
There is eloquence outpouring
When the lion is a-roaring,
And the tiger is a-lashing of his tail!

CHIC.
Yes, I like to see a tiger
From the Congo or the Niger,
And especially when lashing of his tail!

NAT.
Volcanoes have a splendor that is grim,
And earthquakes only terrify the dolts,
But to him who's scientific
There is nothing that's terrific
In the falling of a flight of thunderbolts!

CHIC.
Yes, in spite of all my meekness,
If I have a little weakness,
It's a passion for a flight of thunderbolts!

BOTH.
If that is so,
Sing derry down derry!
It's evident, very,
Our tastes are one.
Away we'll go,
And merrily marry,
Nor tardily tarry

Till day is done!

CHIC. There is beauty in extreme old age—
Do you fancy you are elderly enough?
Information I'm requesting
On a subject interesting:
Is a maiden all the better when she's tough?
NAT. Throughout this wide dominion
It's the general opinion
That she'll last a good deal longer when she's tough.
CHIC. Are you old enough to marry, do you think?
Won't you wait until you're eighty in the shade?
There's a fascination frantic
In a ruin that's romantic;
Do you think you are sufficiently decayed?
NAT. To the matter that you mention
I have given some attention,
And I think I am sufficiently decayed.
BOTH. If that is so,
Sing derry down derry! etc.

(Exeunt together.)

*(Flourish. Enter PANJANDRUM, attended
by FACTOTUM and CHORUS.)*

PAN. Now then, we've had a capital lunch, and we're quite ready.
Have all the painful preparations been made?
FACT. Your Eminence, all is prepared.
PAN. Then produce the unfortunate gentleman and his two well-
meaning but misguided accomplices.

*(Enter CHICO, NATTYSHAW, PRUFROCK, and PATTYCAKE.
They throw themselves at PANJANDRUM'S feet.)*

NAT. Mercy! Mercy for Chico! Mercy for Pattycake! Mercy even
for Prufrock!
PAN. I beg your pardon, I don't think I quite caught that remark.

PRU. Mercy even for Prufrock.

NAT. Mercy! My husband that was to have been is dead, and I have just married this miserable object.

PAN. Oh! You've not been long about it!

CHIC. We were married before the Registrar.

PRU. *I* am the Registrar.

PAN. I see. But my difficulty is that, as you have slain the Heir Apparent—

(Enter HANDY LOU and TRILLIUM. They kneel.)

HAND. The Heir Apparent is *not* slain.

PAN. Bless my heart, my son!

TRI. And your daughter-in-law elected!

NAT. *(Seizing CHICO.)* Traitor, you have deceived me!

PAN. Yes, you are entitled to a little explanation, but I think he will give it better whole than in pieces.

CHIC. Your Eminence, it's like this: It is true I stated that I had killed Handy Lou—

PAN. Yes, with most affecting particulars.

PRU. Merely corroborative detail intended to give artistic verisimilitude to a bald and—

CHIC. *Will* you refrain from putting in your oar? *(To PANJAN-DRUM.)* It's like this: When your Eminence says, "Let a thing be done," it's as good as done—practically, it *is* done, because your Eminence's will is law. Your Eminence says, "Kill a gentleman," and a gentleman is told off to be killed. Consequently, that gentleman is as good as dead—practically, he *is* dead—and if he is dead, why not say so?

PAN. I see. Nothing could possibly be more satisfactory!

FINALE

PAT.   For he's gone and married Trillium—

ALL.   Trillium!

PAT.   Your anger pray bury,

  For all will be merry,

I think you had better succumb—

ALL.   Cumb—cumb.

PAT.   And join our expressions of glee!
CHIC.   On this subject I pray you be dumb—
ALL.   Dumb—dumb!
CHIC.   Your notions, though many,
    Are not worth a penny,
The word for your guidance is "Mum"—
ALL.   Mum—mum!
CHIC.   You've a very good bargain in me.
ALL.   On this subject we pray you be dumb—
                 Dumb—dumb!
We think you had better succumb—
                 Cumb—cumb!
    You'll find there are many
    Who'll wed for a penny,
There are lots of good fish in the sea.
TRI. & HAND. The threatened cloud has passed away,
And brightly shines the dawning day;
What though the night may come too soon,
We've years and years of afternoon!
ALL.   Then let the throng
          {Your/Our} joy advance,
    With laughing song
          And merry dance,
    With joyous shout and ringing cheer,
    Inaugurate {our, your} new career!
          Then let the throng, etc.

CURTAIN

NOTES ON THE NEW NAMES
(LISTED ALPHABETICALLY)

CHICO. *Has been used by but is not limited to one of the Marx Brothers.*

FACTOTUM. *A name for the convenience of the program listing.*

GO-TO. *If and when used, this character is used, his is another name for the convenience of the program listing. (While the idiom no doubt suggested the character's name, when heard onstage it is used as an idiom only, never as a cognomen.) Go-To comes into play when the Pish-Tush can't reach the low notes his madrigal part requires. If the production has a Go-To, he might be listed under as, say, Loman.*

HANDY LOU. *The right number of syllables ending in a sound that necessitates fewer changes to the rhyme scheme. ("Handy Lou" may suggest a change of venue to Whoville; but Whoville is still copyrighted Dr. Seuss territory.)*

NATTYSHAW. *It is my hope that, even accented on the first rather than the second syllable, this will sound more mock-Slavic than mock-Oriental. Incidentally to Gilbert's alleged cruelty to aging females: as a rather ugly old lady myself, I feel not the least bit threatened or insulted because he used for his villainess another rather ugly old lady, inappropriately and ferociously romantic about a man young enough to be her son. Us old ladies are individuals, not a generic.*

PANJANDRUM. *See the poem quoted as an optional Prologue.*

PATTYCAKE. *A name largely for the convenience of the program listing; very seldom heard onstage.*

PRISSY. *Another name for the convenience of the program listing.*

PRUFROCK. *As in "The Love Song of J. Alfred Prufrock," by T. S. Eliot.*

TOBOKU. *Tohu and Bohu were the names Rabelais gave two small fantasy islands in* Pantagruel*; digging further, I discovered that Rabelais must have got them from the Biblical Hebrew "Tohu wa-bohu," which can be* translated *"without form and void."* A *"k"* looked easier to enunciate here than an"h." *It is not unknown for a major city to have the same name as the country in which it is found, nor need the said city even be the country's capital, as New York City is not the capital of New York state.*

TRILLIUM. *As a flower name, this seems appropriate for a heroine, and it is the only two-syllable one ending in 'um that I can think of, even if some of the sung lines do demand creativity with the accent.*